$\mathcal{B}$ODY $\mathcal{L}$ANGUAGE

By C. C. Carter

KINGS CROSSING PUBLISHING

Kings Crossing Publishing – Poetry Division - February 2002

A KINGS CROSSING PUBLICATION
P.O. BOX 673121
ATLANTA GA 30006
KINGSCROSSINGPUB@aol.com

Library of Congress Card Catalog Number: Applied For
ISBN: 0-9714489-1-4

Artistic Direction: LB2, Inc.
Graphic Design by: Robin G. White, Aurellia James
Photography by: Anthony Dowdell
Hair by: Yinka Knight for Mystic Hair Salon & Day Spa
Edited in part by: Cin Salach, Letta Neely, Robin G. White

Printed in the United States of America

BODY LANGUAGE

By C. C. CARTER

Dedicated to

Mama Carter, who taught, spoke, and read poetry to me before I knew that its meaning defined her.

Mom, whose reflection I see daily in my mirror.
Dad, for your Sunday morning sermons.

Yvette, for always and beyond.

Marie... from my window to the furthest star.

Renaé, for 11 p.m. phone conversations while sitting in Walgreens parking lot.

ACKNOWLEDGEMENTS

God is good all the time, all the time God is good!!!!!!

My heart is full and my pen has a stroke so forgive me if I've missed anyone.
My Hot-lanta family - Robin, Sha', Lisa, Leontine
My Big Apple crew - Marie, Anita, Elaine, Rasheeda, Salimah, Diana

ChiTown – you have nurtured and cared for me for seven years as if I were
    one of your own. I have never felt like a stepchild and for that, I will
    love you forever and always claim you as home. It took a village, now
    step back and look at your child.
My papi – Jackie
My mami – Mountain Moving Coffeehouse women
My twin – Cassandra
My sisters – Anitra, Renae, Mary, Lora, Vernita, Evette, Mona, Jessica,
    Susan, Pat, Paula, Donna R, Donna J., Willa, Sharon, Susan, Stacy,
    Tracy, Toni, Kemina, Ronda, Sherri, Chris
My sisters in art – Juarez, Carol, Simone
My sisters in words – Cin, Roiann, Lani, Stacy Ann, Alix, Edith, Tai
    Freedom, Country, Ingrid
My sisters in pen – sharon, Lisa, Kathleen, Letta, Duriel, Maureen
My brothers – Tina, Nancy, K, Sherry
My other brothers _ Shelton, Sanford, Thayer
My brothers in pen – G.Winston, Malik, Reggie, Harry
My brothers in words – Regie, Emanual, Avery, Tony, Victor
My Xs – The studs who taught me to be a woman
My family in theatre – A Real Read
My family in media – Windy City Times, Blacklines, En La Vida,
    Lesbigay Radio
My village in support – The Astraea Foundation, The Literary Exchange,
    Affinity, CBLG, Windy City Black Pride, Zami, Women and Children
    First Bookstore, Star Gaze, Club Escape
My city in appreciation – Every Chi-town venue that let me speak what I
    had to say
My world of women – Every women's festival that exists and those to come.

Dear Butch, Dear Femme, Dear Just You were first published in "Letters to
My Love" chapbook. *Hedonism* was first published in "Best Lesbian Erotica
2000." *On Becoming Woman* was first published in "Dykes With Baggage."

TABLE OF CONTENTS

TABLE OF CONTENTS (cont.)

PROLOGUE

On Becoming Woman

I'm not sure of when it happened, but it was around the time when people stopped calling me cute.

I had stopped shopping in the Misses Department because the cut of a size fourteen didn't become the new shape of my now fuller fourteen woman's hips. So I ventured into the Plus Size Unlimited area and shamefully searched through racks of clothes that years previously I swore would only be for women like my mother. "1X" the tag said, and from the look of the garment that meant they had added extra material – an extra yard to give reason for the plus extra price. And what's with the flowers and sequins placed around the collar? And where are the darts, and tapered waist? I cried as I paid the sales clerk.

At home I had long since given up full length mirrors that revealed soft flesh that used to adorn Venus Williams thighs, Gabrielle's flat stomach, and perfect Halle Berry breasts. A scale that made me the envy of all of my friends, was now a stopper to keep the closet door from swinging shut. Videos of Buns of Steel, Abs of Metal, and Thighs of Stone with little anorexic cheerleaders who didn't need any more exercise than I needed a bowl of ice cream while watching them, had now become bookends for my new collection of self-esteem enhancers.

It wasn't that I didn't care what I looked like, it's just that what I looked like wasn't becoming to me. My idea of perfection had been me at size eight in spandex and three-inch, pumps. Compliments of "You are such a cutie," and "Damn did you see that?" Hot fast sex that lasted for four-hour marathons and still left me saying, "Wait a minute, you aren't done yet are you?"

My lover telling me that I was the cutest little thing that she ever saw – she laying on her back and me draped across her like a mink. These days, I felt that my thighs must feel like tanks pinning her down to the mattress. Many nights I lost sleep because – asleep I couldn't control how heavy to lay on her. Many times I would just roll over onto my stomach and cry inside an arm of flesh. I was constantly reminded of a petite and trim me by pictures wall-papering my bedroom and hallways. And God knows that I dreaded affairs, because that meant nothing to wear, which meant shopping in the fat women's section, again. The final insult to injury was when my high-cut brief panties fit like thongs. And control-top and body-shaper pantyhose were now a necessity even though I wasn't wearing spandex anymore. I resorted to wearing oversized shirts and knits, covering up my not so petite body – hoping people wouldn't notice that I had become unbecoming to them.

One day my lover asked me if I had ever stopped to listen to what people were actually saying. Yeah right, like I wanted to get my feelings hurt all the time. "Girrrrl, how do you get all that ass in them jeans," or "Do you know you got a biiig behind?" My response would be, "You know, I knew it was there when I went to sleep, but sometime between last night and this morning when I got dressed in the mirror I must have forgotten. But thank-you for reminding me."

But OK, one day I took my lover's advice and stopped to listen. Suddenly, I began to notice older mature men glancing at me with smiles, "Sorry I was staring, but you are very pretty." Women stepped aside as I entered parties, and not for the reasons I thought, *God they had to open a space so large because my hips were a sign, "Proceed with caution, wide load approaching."* Instead, I heard things like, "Who is that?" as people asked their friends about me. Those women who braved my response, would approach me and strike up a conversation, usually ending with compliments.

People greeted me with, "Hey sexy. Hello gorgeous." I would look around wondering who they were talking to because, I still dressed in a face-only mirror and always wore oversized clothes.

Yet my lover secretly began replacing my oversized shirts and knits with tailored classic suits and dresses from the Voluptuous Store. That's a name she made up to make me feel good. She took me shopping in the All Women's and Plus Some Departments – buying me fourteen wonderfuls, sixteen wows, and those one extra special sizes. We even found a lingerie store for me that has become my secret – not Victoria's. And now I wear meant to be thongs, bikinis, lace teddies, and bras that don't need miracles because I have developed two of my own.

At night she spoons me from behind – wrapping her arms around my fullness and caressing softness that she swears feels better than the once muscle that kept her head smashed like a rock – putting her face in the folds of my back and cupping breasts whispering, "Damn you feel so good." She turns me over and slowly loves the woman I've become – feeling the maturity in my hips that have spread because I'm now at peak breeding time. She wraps her arms around a waist that can pinch more than an inch, but still indents to form an hourglass, telling the time that it needed to make me this woman.

I call my mother to thank her for not letting this apple roll too far from the tree after it fell.

The scale has been thrown away and full length mirrors unveil a picture of the woman in me. New pictures drape my walls showing me as a girl who happened to be cute – transitioning into pictures that reveal the inner beauty of the woman in me. Lately, I've had to count my blessings and I smile, because, my Womanness Definitely Becomes Me.

PART

I

THE

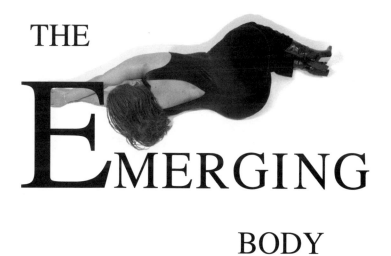

EMERGING

BODY

La Mestiza

My name?
It doesn't matter   neither does my age
On the skin color chart between white and black
        my color is closest to almond beige
        and yet you still wanna call me...
    well you know what you call me

Wrapped in this body of oneness
isamixtureofeveryoneseverythingness
a culture belonging to a particular   nothingness
because I don't have enough anyness   to be defined

Let me explain...
On the census chart I check **OTHER**
Why?
Because I want to
I know all too well what Tiger feels
The majority minority
wanting so bad to call somebody their own
        yet calling me a "sell out" when I refuse to be labeled
        decisively   one way   or   another

Here, call me in the air
"nigger, spic, bati girl, auntie jane"
                        I'm too dark to be white
                        too light to be true black
                        too westernized to identify
                        with my cultural roots

"girl, you'd be a cute sista girl if you'd lock your hair"
                        and too culturally diverse
                        to be considered a true american
"Visa please"

My hips?
Well let's just say my hips
S   p   r   e   a   d
        across two continents
each connected by the sway in my walk
yet keep me from representing
the all american girl on the run ways

Eyes?
That sparkle my bi-racial integration of slavery
make me a photographer's dream

*"Just don't let them see your African ancestral birthmark
between your teeth."*

It's hard carrying africa on my back
europe in my eyes
the west indies in my blood
and spanish *"que corta"* talk on mi tongue
I am more than what you see, what you want to label me

"uno, dos, tres redlight!!"
It's a race…
to see who can label me first…
to stake claim in just that one part of me

"uno, dos, three redlight!!"
I'm not straight enough to be closeted
        not out enough to be gay
        not aggressive enough to be butch
        too much of a lady to be taken seriously

again,
"uno two three redlight!!"
stretching myself to accommodate others
always tugging at the waves of my continents
last time

"one two three redlight!!"
I'm floating in the middle of my MEness
to accept the wonderfulness
of my multicultural mestiza femmeness
yet being enough of a somebody
to label myself
ME

Good Hair

Laticia had long black ponytails
that waved goodbye when she passed

Everyday the four of us
stood at the curb
waited
for her to bounce by
She always had
an entourage close
to the hanging curls –
what we all wanted
and knew as
good hair

Afro Sheen, the blue kind
seeped into scalp
as a hotcomb sizzled at the touch of grease
applied along the nape
of my neck to kitchen naps

Pressing or perming hair
was a necessary evil on Saturday
if we were to get to church by nine on Sundays
I never cared about the ritual
cause I wasn't tenderheaded
and all I could think about
was getting one step closer
to good hair –
even if mama wouldn't let
my braids blow bye in the wind like Laticia's

For two days I
primped in the mirror admiring myself
loving the feel of pink sponge rollers
that would ultimately
reveal nose-length bangs –
the rest parted carefully down the center
without the comb getting stuck
Taking the clear white bauble
twist it around once, twice
click
My three friends and I
stood on the curb
Monday
perpetrating good hair
until the mist from
the rain frizzed up the bangs
then
reminded me
that I was just an average looking black girl
with ancestors
lodged in my roots

Bad Hair Day

I got braids today
Suddenly
I was Black enough for the world to notice
Beautiful enough for **People** to cover

Monday nights   one hour sessions
corn rolling my hair
if I was to get to school on time
Tuesday through Friday
Braids were never pretty   then
they
brown tinsel
twisted into scalps   scarlet symbols
that you had
bad hair
They branded you
black   that wasn't good   or beautiful
especially at ten
when you weren't grown enough
to wear hair out in afro puffs –
not even two or three braids platted
except on picture day and maybe curls on Sunday and Easter
All other days fifty or sixty rows adorned with beads
were worn like armour into daily battles
swinging and slashing at insensitive remarks

Yesterday
I watched   Venus and Serena
slice serves and break barriers

Beads worn like tiaras crowning them champions
Little white boys yelled from stands
fought for a chance to get close
to the cornrolled black beauties   Dredlocked drama
queens
parade across screens in the movie of the week   Fuzzy
wuzzy
doo- wop   Sistahs sing anthems in crowd filled stadiums
and **People**
          name them some of the "Fifty Most Beautiful"
people

So today
I went back to Africa   Beauty Parlor
Told them to make me one of them
of myself
Erase the blond bleach   strip the perm
tired of being invisible
I wanted three hundred braids for two hundred dollars

Later
stepped side ways   heavy headed
but looking good with my
Baaaaad hair
Flicked my switch on   with my twitch on
to whistle wails
and study stares
Yes!!!! Baby!!!!
Black braided and beautiful
That's me!!!!!

The Look

At three she learned the power of the look
when new words of *"mine"* and *"no"* were
powerless beneath the steel hard stares
searing through space until they captured her
attention and threatened of a paddled behind –
from a mother
who refused to let a toddler's tantrums
ruin a perfectly good dinner
or an enjoyable shopping spree at the mall

At 12 she developed the use of the look
when envious teenage girls
rolled eyes and sucked teeth
their words piercing like pins
whenever she walked down the hall –
while pubescent boys not yet mature
physically or mentally
fought to carry her books in an attempt
to win her affection

At 16 she owned the look
while standing on the corner
35th and State in front of the projects
waiting for green to turn red
so she wouldn't be late for school….again
while men her father's age shouted
from rolled down windows
making moving violations
as they violated her innocence
with their obscenities

At 20 she was the object of the look
when a first date went wrong
and the fraternity house captured
her loss of virtue on tape –
viewed it in campus dorms
and watched a young woman with confidence
down grade into self loathing
and degradation

at 25 she became the look –
a blank stare that no one could read
non-emotion walking
while ambitiously working three jobs
attending grad school
sniffing pain, hurt and betrayal through a straw
in an effort to feel something
anything that had been lost
before then –
conceding to parental pressures to be better
than straight As
oblivious to the potential
others saw in her that she couldn't
see in herself

At 30 she defied the looks of others
when she "suddenly turned gay"
because no one saw it coming
and *"it must be a result of what happened in college"*
so this phase will pass
she will begin therapy
so that this problem can be fixed

and *"what will our friends think?,"*
she looking past people's perception
in an effort to save her life
and secure her own happiness

At 35 she appreciates the looks of the past
incorporates them into her daily life of today
as she raises children –
uses it to control
the temperament of her two-year-old –
acknowledges it when her pre-teen
comes home from school
hating the world and her pre-mature
hormonal growth –
embraces it when her lover
sends waves from thirty feet across
a crowded room –
and works with other women
who have become the objects of it –
helping them to brush off the stares
teaching them to create barricades
make ammunition
and recognize the power
they have with just one look

No Gap-Toothed Blues

Everyday I step through g a p s
except the one   between my teeth
I've managed to fill *s* **g** *p* a *c* **p** *e* s
on the job, not quite touching the ceiling
but close
to my lover
I fill the gap in her heart
so we become
bonded   teeth is what the dentist says I need
I lie back on soft cushion –
white interrogation light
shines bright in my pupils
He places a pencil eraser
between my g a p
sucks air through his own   in disgust
He wants to barb wire them   fence them behind brackets
squeeze shut with pliers   add a fake piece
to erase the only visible
sign of my ancestral tribe
left   a cd plays billie
singing the blues
what does he know about heartache
yet he says I must sing
often because the size of my   **g**   **a**   **p**
should make me cry –
A clay mold plastered
across no cavitied teeth and gums   he hums
I need to spit   out
sterilized white smocks
hands, lights and enameled teeth
cause my gap don't sing no blues

when I smile
it's contagious   curiosity to see what's
between
the **g   a   p**
draws you into the journey
and it sings –
my bi coastal ancestors
          merge
and dance in this space
my lover and I become
one
when we meet in this space
my signature is sealed
of who I am
where I came from
where I'm going   out of here in this space
He says we'll start the process
of bracing this g-a-p
next week
when the mold is examined
I know
I will not return   so I
wipe my mouth with white tissue
smile wide saying "yes"   thinking "no"
swipe the pencil for a souvenir
turn
left   sing with billie
my NO – **g   a   p**   tooth blues
song

Scarred at Birth
(for Betty)

She thinks
the scar

s

l

i

c

i

n

g

down her stomach
makes her unworthy to wear the term   woman
more from a battle lost than one won

I don't think
the seven-pound fifteen-ounce   warrior
who fought tangled umbilical cord
for twenty-one hours
                    wrapped like ivy vines
around his neck and chest
sending stressed s-o-s heartbeats
into a monitor because he wanted to live
would think
his   life giver
a failure
for giving him first breaths

I think
he will think   her great the way he

will be
not because he did not
begin life
s
   l
     i
       p
         ping down a vaginal canal
screaming, hollering and breathing
like a passed kidney stone –
but more like giving her "A"
for having vision to C-section him clear
from danger
She
will be in his eyes   a queen
who birthed a king
I don't think
that makes her less   woman
any more than she   my
lover's birth   child
makes me less
    her

                    mother

Sign Language

Your fingers now intertwined with mine
remind me of the first time
you took my hand in yours –
we walked quietly
letting the wind swing our arms
back and forth   Then
talking seemed an unnecessary act –
we shared more through silence
and innocent touch
then we ever could
from nervous conversation
You got to know
my thoughts
by the way
my palms would sweat
my fears
by the way I tightened our grip
when we passed stray dogs
my desire
when I took my thumb
lightly brushed it against the inside
of yours
You first told me
you loved me
by putting your hands under mine
bringing them to your lips
kissed each finger
as if taking sacred communion
Now as we cross the street
you take mine in yours
I wonder if I squeeze it back
or am reluctant to let go
will you understand what it is
I'm trying to say

Lil' Girl Black

In a black cap sleeved leotard
blush stretch tights and pink slippers
s-curved at ten, unable to hide genetics
I am a vulnerable target   *Her*
pointer – my smacked thigh
a constant reminder
"Don't arch your back, Miss Carter"
that a ballerina - I ain't
Tucking this history is hard
"Demi plie and straight, demi plie and straight"
4/4 tempo without base is no encouragement
Inside my head bongos and congas
call me home
"Loose bodies do not belong in my class"
watusi and shango
want possession of my legs
allowed only to form arabesque, and piques'
"No, no your lines are all off"
so it's
"Pirouette and lift, pirouette and lift"
I do not soar like eagles
nor glide like water
I am not tight like cement
nor controlled like power
"Do not contract your shoulders, Miss Carter"
I stay grounded
and swirl like color blended
black
my corn rolls click a metronome for time
"You must learn to spot"
and I do - spot where I belong

"Not before you pass my class"
across the hall
black leotards draped in kente cloth
plus four djembe sing my anthem –
bent legs and loose hips are allowed to cause earthquakes –
bodies conjure up history –
claiming Africa is a prerequisite for that class –
I plot when to escape
and join the mother ship
but for now it's
"Pas de bourre'e, pas de bourre'e, rond de jambe and bow.
That's much better Miss Carter"
"Whatever it takes," I say
Whatever it takes.

26 Years of Incarceration

My thighs have been victims
of body profiling
since the eighth grade –
Locked and chained in lycra
and nylon
gasping for air
suffocating
while wishing for escape
no release
afraid to breathe
anymore
fear of freedom
too close to grasp –
they wish to run loose
under satin and rayon
walk while rumbling
beneath denim and twill –
show no shame for the
cellulite-covered flesh
that would dance open
in sunlight
if only they belonged
to a body
size 4

That's what society has taught them

That they are not beauty –
nor sexy or healthy
They are sights
for blind eyes

So we find them guilty of treason
Sentence them to a minimum twenty-six years
to life
of spandex solitary confinement
for being too big
too bulky
too other than
size sports illustrated model
size vogue magazine cover
size soap opera star
size movie leading lady

Treat them like convicts on death row
strap down
starve thin
then in a desperate attempt to plea bargain
we cardio them light weight
pump them steroid
lipo suck them skinny
All to make them
acceptable for the civilized world
So little kids who see them
in the pool
in a swimsuit
don't point and say
"oooh mommy look
at the lady with the cottage cheese legs"

Footprints in the Sand
(Sunday morning at Michigan Womyn's Music Festival)

heel
toe
stomp brush
brush
stomp
heal toe
kick ball change
brush brush
stomp
mean nothing…
bare foot in red dirt
conditioned response
to feel rhythm leave
here
amongst women who dance
free
naked in woods
flat feet, unpolished toes
leave prints
i step into their legacies –
Beneath blazing sun
in one-ten degree heat
orange bra, soon none
red, pink, purple sarong
draped loosely
low enough to let gold chastity belt show
open enough to let thighs breathe
short enough to let feet flutter
i dance in sand
sweat pouring like rain
draws a circle for women

to kneel
clap
clap chant
snap snap sing
clap chant snap sing
clap
chant
sing
while watching
my feet create music in earth –
grains stick between crevices
embedded in heel
toe
stomp
Drums like thunder, voices like mother
feet clear paths for others to join
brush brush
stomp
each one leaves one
footprint
in the sand
we follow one another
sink into each others
leave traces to follow the journey
kick
ball change
kick ball change
stomp
stomp
stomp

PART

II

THE

Evolving

BODY

Your Entrance

There are times when you
walk into a room
I faint between breaths   lose
sight to others but see you
mute to my own voice   but then
come back to my senses   stick
out my chest
peacocked
and say,
"Oh her? That one's with me"

Dear Butch,

for keeping your nails filed down
and manicured, while insisting
that mine stay long polished and glossed

for wearing boxers and a t-shirt
to bed and buying me
lace and satin nighties

for shopping in the men's department
and watching them hesitate
before showing you into the fitting room

for men giving you hi-fives after realizing
I'm with you – for women sneaking sly smiles
after realizing you're with me

for staring at me like I might disappear
if you blink, for holding me like
I am a memory remembered

for having a soft touch contrasted to your demeanor
for making love to me as two genders with one body like mine
and crying with me when we become one

for being strong like we were told
men were supposed to be   for being sensitive
like we know women can be

for standing up to the hims
when they attack the mes
for being with the yous

for being enough man so that I don't need one
for being all woman
because that's why I'm with one

for all the times you've asked how some women
turn out to be you   Thanks for answering
why some women are born me

All my Love

F e m m e

Dear Femme

for wearing two inch heels
with nineteen inch skirts
and making me wear shoes
with my dress pants

for keeping your seams straight
down the back of sheer hose
and making sure all my socks have a gold toe

for wearing matching miracle bra
and panty sets every day
while I wear boxers my way

for not buying me frilly blouses
to go with my suits and not insisting
that I wear lipstick for a disguise

for never seeming to be embarrassed
by the looks we get in restaurants

for holding my hand in public
and kissing me good-bye
when I drop you off at work

for allowing me to be the partner
that your parents would have picked

for being the spouse that my parents
thought I'd never have

for being the mother of my brother's child
so that we can have a family of our own
and never letting me slouch on my parental duties

for not being afraid to roll me on my back
whenever I forget that I'm a woman

for calling me "papi" in the heat of the moment
when you knew then that I wished I were one

for all the times you've thought that I thought
you needed to be more like me

Thank-you for being you

and loving the masculine
woman in me

always with love,

Butch

Non-Gendered Girl

My lover hates the label   "lesbian"
being called "butch" even more
doesn't identify as trans –
She prefers non-gendered
knowing that genetics
the second x
beating out the one y
in a race toward the egg
interfered with god's plan
So she suffers through this life   walking
fine   lines
between
genders –
what she feels
and who she really is
Taking questioning glances
as people do double takes
at the   boy with the girlish face
as confirmation of god's original intent –
Praying nightly that her return to next life
will be   in the body
this life disguises   in female form –
Her only saving grace from entering
next life by her own hand is coming
home daily to the   straight
lesbian wife
who understands her daily hell
and loves unconditionally
the man   trapped
           inside
              of this
                 woman

The Otherside of Taboo

I am often criticized for loving a woman
who dresses like a man
Open to attacks of
  "Maybe subconsciously you want to be with one"
My response?
At 5
I remember
2 barbies and one ken...
undressing him and dressing one of her
    in his black leather jacket and faded studded jeans
calling the two girls a couple
    ken...
    their maid
at 10
playing house with the next door neighbor...
    a girl
  who wore boys sport shorts
    a baseball hat hiding a ponytail
    her older brother's tanked t-shirt
    not needing a sports bra
            then...
  who had to be the daddy and I
        the only girl
    willing to play wife ...to her
at 15
joining the girl's softball team...even though I couldn't hit
  just because the smell of sweat
      girl funk from a hot summer game
      on the bus back to school
  was better then the scent from
      perfumed drenched
      femme girls on the cheerleading squad of which
I was the captain

at 18
attending every college girl's basketball game…
often the only one in the stands…
back then…
cheering my lungs out as an excuse to scream my frustration
                              a disguised cry for help
              not understanding why my fascination for
a girl
          who   played like a boy
                 bopped like a Westside thug
                 cursed like a sailor
          kept   me
sniffing like a cat in heat
                 made my loins ache so…
                 and not knowing other
                 girls
          who   looked liked me
          who   wanted girls like them…
to form a support group for help

at 22
almost marrying
                 a man
          who   wore Brooks Brother's suits
                 smelled like musk mixed with Obsession
                 swooned me with strong grip and soft touch
                 satisfied me with good love making…
but whose   masculinity
alone

                              couldn't keep
                                                me
from   walking to the other side toward
                                           a woman
who   wore men's tailored shirts and pants
         held me with a safe embrace
         caressed me with light kisses
         loved me with insatiable desire... and
                                   whose body
                          the same as my own
keeps me
forever suspended
                      on the
                         forbidden   side of   taboo
                            even within my own
                                             lifestyle

Dear Just You

for not being a top searching for a bottom
or a bottom looking for a top
but for being a woman loving women
and meeting me horizontally where it counts

for wearing a suit to work in the morning
your hat to the back on the court
a gown to the ball in the evening
and nothing but your womaness to bed at night

for keeping your hair wrapped
wig weaved, dreds locked, afro puffed
head shaved, bob cut, perm straight
all within a month cause that's just you

for not having restrictions
on what I can and cannot do
when I roll you over or work from under
cause you know that one on one
as two women, it's all good

for being an "either or" when you want to
and a "neither nor" when you don't
but always being you
cause you are

for not giving yourself any other label
but the one you call
"woman"   yet crowning me
with the title "Queen"

for being the invisible ones in our community
but the important ones that made our history

for all the times you've thought
you've been misunderstood
underrepresented
and totally disrespected

Thank-you for not heeding to the pressures
of identifying with a category
other than the one I label
"Just You"

All my love,

Just Me

Slowly We Merge

It starts with a look
fingers tracing desire
across lips until they quiver
A head tilted back   kisses and neck
greet each other a familiar hello
Hands read braille down shoulders   One
resting where waist and hips meet
the other searching flesh under shirt
finding a hook then pop with index and thumb
Breathy moans to ourselves when chest meet breasts
Flesh heating like black tar on sun scorched streets
Ears tuned to the gasp of air that prevents passing out
Hands soul searching –
a thigh wrapped over leg   cross twined
face to face   chest to breast   stomach to pelvis
thigh to knee   calf to toe   scissored
we move
prisoners to the feeling
the only escape are the
yes'   oh god's   umh's and   ahh's
uncontainable
phrases that do no justice to the word
sex
when it's women loving women
we press harder
sweat sizzling
with touch
hands signing I love you
down spines   up thighs   between cleavage
amongst bodies
until hands   touch
where womanhood and spirit
live

and slowly we merge   like **harmonyandmelody**
when the rhythm is just right
we merge   like   **winterintospring**
overnight with the migration of the winds
we merge   like   colors in the spectrum
spinning in circles
casting out light
except the one that we see in each others eyes
we merge   like   **walkingintowaves**
sinking with each step
until water covers head
drowning in each otherness
we merge   like   **scienceandmath**
an equation of numbers with infinite possibilities
unless divided by itself
1 into 1 will always   be
we merge   like
deathintolife
the cycle of I am
passing from elder to child
where one ends another begins
together
we merge
god into soul   body into flesh
butch into femme   them into us   you into me
woman
into woman
we
merge
one

When You Hold Me

We become foreign phrases that
journey toward a common dialect

I burn but   wait
for the message inscribed in your hands
to write a love letter around my waist
send a SOS down my spine
sing a song along my legs
teach my body how to speak
in tongues

PART

III

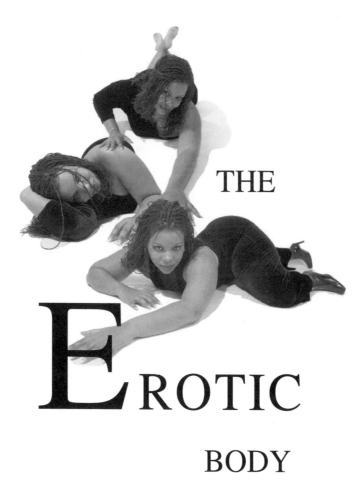

THE

Erotic

BODY

Hedonism 1992

i'm, i'm thinkin, i'm thinkin bout, i'm thinkin bout missed
opportunity
i'm thinkin bout missed opportunity with you

i'm thinkin bout
breakfast at ten
a table set for four
laced white on solid oak
your skin and wood contrast
to smothered antique ceramics
the smell of hot croissants
layered with dripping cheese
spiced butter, two kinds
cinnamon and plum
a bowl full of mixed fruits
melons, kiwis and blueberries
a compote cream to glaze them in

i'm thinkin bout
how I want
to lie across laced linen
give myself to you
as a sacrificial offering
bless me
like you praise the food
part my legs
like you peel layered croissants
pour cream over my body
like you drench the fruit
taste honey dew
now all sweet and ripe

melt over me like cheddar
until I bubble

spread your loving across
my body
churning butter
two kinds
your flavor and mine
but i'm thinkin …
there's a table
set for four
so we're not alone
just me and u
and my thinkin
has to be enough for now

it's late evening
same table
we sit
eye to eye
lip to lip
talking –
i'm thinkin bout
how I want to tell you
to love me
like you worship your dreds
start with the hair on my body
that is unpermed
part it into sections
take some strands
slip a thumb inside my bees wax
twist my wet emotions
around your index finger
until i'm molded into locks
but i'm thinkin…
femme etiquette
doesn't allow for such honesty

what would you think
of me thinkin like this?
so i'm thinkin
this is another missed opportunity with you

i'm thinkin bout
a kitchen counter
where you kiss me
I inhale your tongue
exchanging breaths
slowly in the beginning
until our lips make 1+1=1
i'm thinkin bout
the "umh" you moan
when they finally touch
how if I wasn't conditioned
at being a "Miss Thang"
I would tell you
to bend me over this counter
so we can begin doing
"that thang"
kiss the other lips
with the same "umh"
that you are breathing into these
stir with a finger, a spoon, a ladle
or whatever else you could find
cause the kitchen
is as good a place as any
to cook you up some shit
but i'm thinkin...
the inn keepers get up at five
and it's four thirty
so breathing in kisses
has to be enough for now

i'm thinkin bout
the irony of the Garden Room
your room
where you unfasten
my chastity belt
claim it yours
i bite the apple
no seduction required
we recognize our nakedness
no shame admitted
we love each others bodies
the same is required
the granddaughter
of a Caribbean Indian
and the legacy
of a Dominican Servant
rewrite Genesis –
In the beginning
there was eva
created from red clay
and eve
was taken from her breast –
they were crowned
butch and femme
and given the queendom of goddess
but i'm thinkin…
that's not what really happened
just what i'm thinkin
but given another opportunity
I won't be thinkin
you won't be guessin
cause we will be doin

Baby Talk

She calls me Baby
the word t
      r
        i
          p
            s   off
her tongue
stops me short stride
makes me moon walk
sdrawkcab backwards
into the   empty space
between her arms and cradles
baby crawls out like yawns
mid morning
smells like us last night
ooooozzzzzed out of black
bodies onto soaked sheets
sounds like somebody's
baby cries   kisses on
my shoulder
heads for cleavage
to comfort tears
calm her heart's
baby beats   the blues
when she's lonely   away
I can hear   baby tunes
tap in my mind makes me
pick up the phone
dial the number
to my Baby's
baby talk
to me

Sweet Tooth

She says my Sweetness
soothes her sweet tooth
non-artificial flavor
no saccharin or sweet and low
I keep her high
naturally
Jamaican grown
brown sugar cane planted
in Santa Domingo soil
imported to the Mississippi
south harvested for thirty five
years in scorching sun
picked at peek replacing
those not equal to my honey
packaged pretty
delivered to her table
karo light and molasses thick –
makes her mind syrupy
gets her fingers sticky
keeps her tastes craving
confection blended
non granulated
100% blessed
by
birth
sugar

Kiss Me

Kiss me like I'm ice cream
your favorite flavor melting on your tongue
teasing tastebuds while sliding down your throat
numbing stomach pains with a brain freeze
wet, sticky and sloppy
wiping your mouth with the back of your hand
ahhhhhhhhhhhh

Kiss me like you've just remembered an "Old School" tune
in a blue lit basement
up against a wall
get it quick but make it good
cause mom flicks on the light at twelve
and then the party's over and I become
the memory of the good ole days
that you hummmmmm

Kiss me like I've gone into cardiac arrest
dying slowly in your arms
sinking fast into never knowing who you were
Perform CPR to revive me
your breath filling my lungs with
"I'll never let you leave me" desperation
until you get a pulse
feel the beat of my heart
then hear me murmur
mmmmmmmm, I know I am alive

Kiss me like we invented the word
perfected the touch of the tongues
patented the feel of the lips
concocted the mixture of moans
two sets of lips mistaken as one
and we don't know whose is whose
cause they've dissolved into each other's
ooooohhhhhhhhhhhhhh, yes

Kiss me like you'd kiss yourself if you could

Sleepwalking

...is second nature
for hands that creep
subconsciously
between the crevice of my
thighs while she dreams

her body
spooned like puzzle pieces
behind me
her breath
steady beats
of air on my back
sounds like wind seeping
through cracked windows
her hands
awake and curious
starved for affection
or cold and need heat
caress me awake
tracing the lines of silhouette
like taking a picture imprinted
in her palms
from leg
to thigh
to hips
to waist
to shoulder
they travel –
light brushes
up then
down
until her breath
in my back
turns to a quiet snore

her hands
pull me tighter
lie across my waist
then
settle down and rest –
a nightly ritual
while she sleeps

Lady-Like

I was raised to be a lady
sent to ballet and dance classes at four
charm school at ten
There I learned to sit up straight
cross my legs
lock them at the ankles
Never raise my voice above a whisper
nor wear red which was for whores

In church I learned
        not to take the Lord's name in vain
        be faithful, know God, and keep the Sabbath Holy

I played like a child
        but did so in pink lace dresses and
        white trimmed bobby socks –
Never heard me screaming out the window to my friends
or down the block from one end to the other
Did not fight like other girls
        scratching and clawing
        for the affection of a boy
Didn't use foul words
        flowing out the mouths of other kids
        like foreign language too familiar for their tongues

In college
        I read Emily Post's book of Etiquette
        as religiously as my Bible
        both still on my nightstand next to the bed
Even learned to love through technique
        suppressing feelings of lust and passion
                         both sins

for expertise in missionary positions
that surrendered myself to their pleasure
                    alone
For that
        I received my merit badge and colonel stripes
        from potential suitors whose goals
        were corporate conquests and
        political penetrations on their way up the ladder
        to success

Then I met you
        Who through touch and taste of skin
                made me bury my lady-like demeanor
        Who likes to watch others watch my hips switch
                when I walk away
        Who pays for me to get my nails and toes
                painted Little Corvette Red
        Who likes me to sit up straight
                when you're strapped
                while my hips dance up and down
                back and forth
                you playing hide and seek in my wetness
Who likes to hear my lady-like moans
        turn into woman words
        after teaching me new vocabulary
        foul language that flows off my tongue
                no longer foreign to me
The F words
        Finger
        Fist
The S words
        Suck
        Stroke

The D words
        Deeper
        Damn it
The G word said in vain
        Oh God!!
And in mid thrust
        You stop and say
        "Girl quit calling on the man
        he ain't making you come like this
        I am
        You gonna call somebody
        Say my name"
Red polished fingers skate down your back
like skis on snow banked hills
leaving trails across your shoulders
on the way down
Both hands cupped on my cheeks
        your face embedded in my neck
My legs wrapped around your waist
        not forgetting what charm school taught
        crossed at the ankles
You say
        "What's my name girl?"
                "Boy"
        "What's my Name?"
                "Butch"
        "What's MY Name?"
                "Ai Papi"
        "Yes!! Girl say my name!"
                "DADDY!!"
        "Yes, Say it!!"
                "That's It!!"
        "Say IT!!"
                "RIGHT THERE!!"
        "SAY IT!!!"

Emily Post falls off the night stand
    she's rolling over on the floor
The Bible knocked over
    conveniently opens to Song of Solomon
    love letters to Basheba are
    confirmation that this kind of love
    united countries with controversy
    even back then

I scream
    not giving a shit about protocol and etiquette
    or the fact that I am catholic
Or if
    when I see my neighbor in the morning
    will she look at me and roll her eyes in jealousy
    cause a woman loved me better than her husband
    has ever done in their whole 15 year marriage
    making three babies
    and out of all that she still hasn't had one good
Headboard banging, bedspring shrieking, sheet staining, body
soaking, feet and leg trembling, hips and pelvic pumping,
scratching and clawing, new permed hair sweating completely
out, word spatting like you need an exorcism
Type of come

And when we're through
    soiled pink and lace panties thrown across the room
    are a reminder of my up bringing

Like I said
    I was raised to be a lady
    then I met you
and learned how to be a woman

Just Before Morning....

the after scent of our frolicking dreams

taps morning on the shoulder
"come, rise once more"
the heat between bodies escapes –
a new breeze creeps through my thighs -

turning to brush against your pre-dawn rise
I breathe coupled aromas.

You feel the wetness
of my morning dew
created late
after melting
it's midnight frost.

when night and morning meet
so do we
mixing dew drops
awaiting the explosive

sunrise

I Want To Go Back

I want to go back to the beginning

When everyday with you
seemed like the last day of school
and every weekend was spring break

When saying my name
sounded like the only love song
and every love song reminded me of you

I want to go back

When night stars spelled out your name
and day clouds formed your face

When below fifty degrees
felt like plus one hundred
just because you touched my hand

I want to go back

When the vibrations of my pager
made me smile because your code was 69
and having a car phone was an excuse

to say "I'm in the neighborhood...Can I see you?"

When every hour of the day was 4:00 - our time
and every minute was 3:59 before you came home

I want to go back
To the Me and the You
before everyone else got into the We
When there was an unspoken obligation of Us
and the status of Two did not need to be defined
because it was understood that I and You Are

I want to go back

When dinner was each other and dessert
was that we made it to the bedroom this time
When you got drunk with the thought of drinking me
and I got high at the thought of being on top

I want to go back

When we were always late to affairs
because where we were going had no importance
                              of where we had just come from

I want to go back

To creating new beginnings that never
become middles and end with no conclusions
I want everyday to be an unconscious newness
like summer recess and kindergarten playtime
I don't want to recreate old beginnings –
what I want is to re-begin daily with you

PART

IV

THE

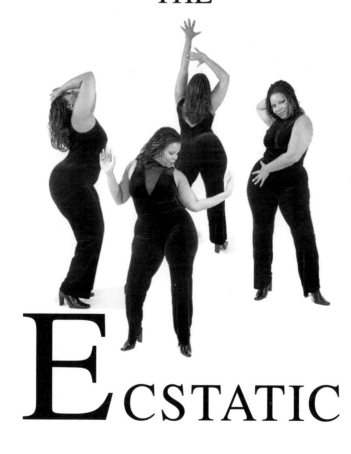

E CSTATIC

BODY

Women Are Music

Women are clef notes
on stacked bars
played on fingered ivories
blown by tongued reeds
each works to create music that whisper or scream
a song you want to hear

We have a sound for all ears
fit into categories for all types
whatever mood is your desire
we are the rhythms of your delight

Jazz is a woman let loose
to run wild in violet draped orchid fields
arms flinging melody
feet dancing percussion
locks blowing harmony
body scatting time
to the tune of firework blasts
on a fourth of July night

Blues be bent bodies
in still birthed love
whaling out labor pains
from breached abandonment
miscarried devotion
premature commitment
broken
bared breasts promises

We are Rap
on the corner of 79th and Cottage
sucking teeth
twirling one braid
rolling four eyes
talking to the back of a hand
never stop giving praise
when on our back
legs squeezed tight
keeping time with our own rhythm

We are
hallelujah hymns and praise god gospels
testifying in tongues   while
healing hands save sinning souls
shaking for salvation   Our
love making
taking us one step closer to heaven

We are the ballads that lullaby you
caressing brows with bosom
and pillowed lyrics

We are classical symphonies
playing violin concertos
stringing you along
arranging your thoughts
as each movement develops

We are the unforgettable tunes you hum
when cruising the radio searching
to find that one song that describes us

We are music videos that keep
you channel surfing when more than
one of us are in a room

We are Italian Operas
Country and folk yodels
Spanish and Taino rhythms
Reggae and Calypso tempos

We are the rock that keeps you steady
and the roll that makes you gyrate
to the motion hypnotically in time with us

We keep you dancing our bodies
and singing our songs
clapping your hands and stomping your feet
as we twist and turn you on

We are universal music disguised as women

Thousand Waves

Feeling less than who I am
                    a woman

I pamper myself today
"A Special" at a Thousand Waves Day Spa
So I take advantage

I haven't been feeling myself
                    a woman

Too short, too fat, too this, too that
A massage is what I need

In the dressing room
embarrassed to be naked
The other women
                    toned and buffed
My muscles submerged beneath cellulite

I wait for them to leave
holding my breath with anxiety
of how I used to look like that
I pull out my swimsuit
me naked has to wait another day
I undress to get dressed
avoid the mirror
even my eyes don't like what they see
                    a woman
Who used to be

Somebody's watching

But I am alone

Somebody's staring

But nobody's here

To my left on a wall
Hangs a picture
                    a woman

One breast the other scarred
She stands naked

Watching

Her eyes disappointed
I turn from the stare
gaze on a poster of Audre
and lord why do you do this to me?
Fist raised, head wrapped
she hollers through trance
I, as if hypnotized
remove clothes covering flesh
stand naked before the mirror

                    see a woman
No courage though
I dress
I leave
I go home

                    to a woman
Who makes love to my body
But has never seen me naked

Full flesh
Full figured
    full woman

Happy I'm home
she kisses me deeply
holds me tightly
raises my skirt
and enters me gently

I'm drifting on a motionless sea
but remember
this too leads to being naked
I stop
run into the bedroom
hide under the covers
wait for her to follow
she falls on soft flesh

She wants to see me bare
    she never has
Wants to see what she feels when she loves me
    a woman

I've never let her

But the tide rises in the sea
Mermaids haunt my thoughts

The woman who makes love to my body
has breasts she wishes she didn't
but loves mine which I wish were
More full
More round
More firm

More feeling!!!

Her tongue teases nipple

They respond
But I don't
I have never known the pleasure
Some other women feel
I close my eyes and try
yet the mermaids swim toward the shore
invade our private moment
remind me of my cowardness
----of my selfishness
----of my
----my

and Audre at one side
fist raised
head wrapped

Screaming!!!

While the woman who makes love to my body
Whispers

You are not alone

Oooooh you feel so good

You are not a quitter

Ooooh you sound so good

You are the torch carrier

Ooooh you taste so good

tongue teases nipple
and I begin to feel

and yes you can feel!!

and damn you feel sooooo good!!

The mermaids
and the woman
who loves my body
make me come alive
a thousand waves send the tides
slapping
rippling
flowing through body
pouring on sheets

for those who feel no more

for those who will no more

for those after me to invent the cure

to be a woman

and in the morning
I lay naked beside the woman
who loves me not just my body
my gaze follows her arm
that drapes across the waist
of my womanish body
The mermaids are gone
but echo in ears
I turn to the woman

who loves me and my body
shake her awake
stand up in all my
cellulite covered muscle
small soft breasts
pouched childless stomach
thick bushed hair
spread my arms wide
And hollar
"Here you go, Baby
Take Me As I Am!!!!!!"

The Herstory Of My Hips

What is it that you misunderstand about these hips?
my hips?
These are my hips-
these 52-inch hips
attached to this 36-inch waist
are my hips and they tell herstory

perhaps you question the size of my hips
the second largest continent in the world sired these hips
of course they would be as large

the oldest civilization on earth gave birth to these hips
of course they would be as wide

for these were my great grandmother's
and my grandmother's
and my mother's hips
and now I am heir to this throne – my crown?
these hips of course
and I will proudly pass them on to my daughter
for her dowry

These hips are pyramids-
no blueprints modern technology
no cranes and chains erected these hips
blood sweat and joy created these hips

My West Indian "fadder"
loved my Dominican "madre"
and they mixed up the spices
to create the recipe for these hips

cause my hips are hip-
they swing a jazz tune
they bop a blues beat
they talk a rap rhythm
they dance a drum solo

these are hot summer day
cold winter nights
spring into action
make you fall in my lap hips-

These are my hips-
no aerobics
no treadmills
no run a mile
these hips are for you to snuggle
for you to cuddle
for you to sink into and dream
for you to get lost in all your fantasies
wrap yourself around and let me squeeze you hips
lock you in and yell "si mami" hips
draw you deeper so you can scream,
"dame ah bueno, dame ah bueno," hips
shake with ecstasy, "what's my name?" hips
rock your world and swing from chandelier hips
make you release before you were ready to hips

So, when you want to hold a woman's hips
when you want to feel the difference between you and me hips
when hard hips want to be soothed by Charmin hips
Come over to these hips
and let the legacy live on.

Turning 40

At 10   I thought
forty was some wicked woman number
that transformed girls into their mothers
where sharp cutting edge, hip-hop words and language
were replaced with phrases like
"When I was your age..."
and my wardrobe would have to come
from the "Women as old as me must act like ladies
and dress totally conservative" department

at 20   I thought
forty was this mythical middle aged number
that magically made you
financially secure, totally grounded
and unthinkably settled
faint smiles hiding
memories of things that you thought
you should've done
where you could've gone
who you would've been
if only you knew at twenty what you know now

at 30   I thought
forty was this fast approaching catch up number
that echoed a constant whisper in your ear
to start getting your act together
before you don't have an act to get
that dauntless conversations be replaced
with lingo about IRA, CYA and
who I met at AA
or some other self-help therapy group

but now at 40
I'm finding out that
this age be some
secret initiation into true womanhood number
that separates me from
twenty something stupidity
and elderly senility
I've arrived
like a warrior
with battle scars and armour
ready to fight my way into the prime of my life
for now, 40 has new meaning for me

40 be me – a chocolate covered
universe walking this earth
with two galaxies
swirled around brown sugar milky ways
pointing south toward my big dipper
enticing you to make a wish

40 be me – a shooting star
blazing across sky
reflecting off water
and shining in flesh
a goddess light burning in woman soul

See I'm redefining what 40 means
to be a walking bill board for those
apprehensive to open
the main entrance into their life

Together me and my other
forty-something sisters
re-shape the term middle age
redirect the stereotypes
and re-create the images
that our teen daughters see
that our twenty somethings think
that our thirty approachings dread
Today I am forty and this is the first day
of the rest of my life

There Is A Spirit

There is a spirit
Moving …   There is a spirit
    Moving…   There is a spirit
        Moving…   There is a spirit
                In Me…

from the top of my head to the bottom of my feet
the tip of my fingers the curl of my toes
rushing through me like water over rock
smoothing out the rough edges
a tidal wave in motion of flesh
splashing against bones
making me sway to the tune of its echo

There is a spirit there is a spirit there is a spirit
moving moving moving in me... listen
to a body speaking in tongues
hands singing a prayer of amens
arms embracing a hug from the sky
back arching to hold up the sun and shadow the moon
hips dancing the lambada with the wind
feet kissing the earth with thanksgiving

There is a spirit there is a spirit there is a spirit
moving moving moving
in me…
body language created from ancient voices

of caribbean nannies
european au pairs
dominican midwives
african slaves

moving moving moving
spreading me open to the earth
a diamond for the world to appraise
a gift for mother nature to inhale
a temple for my grandmothers mother and my daughters to
dwell
a sanctuary for the goddesses to pray
a spirit a spirit a spirit moving moving moving
sssssssshhhhhhhhhhhhhhhh…

playing ancient rhythms with future lullabies
of days gone by and nights to come
moving moving moving
Listen to the beat of my breasts
the songs singing in my eyes
the lyrics from the caress of my hands
the melodies from the brush of my shoulders
there is a spirit
in the sway of my walk
the tenacity of my talk
the persistence in my steps
the essence of my breath
ahhhhhhhhhhhhhhhh

There is a spirit there is a spirit there is a spirit
moving moving moving there is a spirit
there is a spirit there is a spirit forming forming
forming there is a spirit there is a spirit there is a spirit
growing growing growing there is a spirit
there is a spirit
there is a spirit
yelling
calling
naming me…
WOMAN

I'm A God Thang

I am
You are
We are
God thangs
I am   you are
We are
God thangs
I am   you are   we are
god thangs
I am you are we are god thangs
I'm a god thang
a walking talking breathing speaking
miracle thang
a descendant from all of the her thangs
the daughter of the dawn of Eve thang
I'm the life of the original woman thang
you know?
a god thang

If it's true that my life was prescribed
before I was born
than I am a no mistake god thang

If it's true that she is all knowing
and my destiny was written
once I was conceived
than I am a meant to be me god thang

If she blew her breath into
felons and sex offenders
cult leaders and adulterers
than surely
the creator of no evil

made me too   the least of all sinners
to be a God Thang

If I can travel to many countries
study various cultures
translate foreign languages
and speak eclectic tongues-
hang with the west side
chill on the south side
cyber-space to the north side
commute from the east side
with people far and near
who are doing their thang   like I do my thang-
than I am a city slicking
nation nobbing
world wide webbing
God Thang

I'm a
C.C.   Etta
Maimie   Genevieve
Little Mama
Sojournor Truth   Harriet Tubman
Nzinga   Nefertti
Basheba Ruth
Mary   Eve
God Thang

So who are you to question
how and why God does her thang?
If you have a problem with me
and the way I do my thang
May I suggest you
take it up with the head
MS. THANG!

ABOUT THE AUTHOR

C.C. CARTER earned her M.A. in Creative Writing from Queens College in New York. She is a graduate of Spelman College in Atlanta, receiving her B.A. in English Literature. This year she will be a judge and celebrity guest at the 2002 Gay Games in Sydney, Australia. She is the author of a chapbook, Letters to My Love. However, she can be seen touring the Women's Music Festival circuit, performing from her poetry and prose work, "Living Large In A Shrinking America." The once aspiring actress, now moonlights as one, and can be seen in the film documentary, *Living With Pride – Ruth Ellis @100 Years, Kevin's Room,* and *Chic-a-go-go Children's Hour.* She is a member of the Performance Ensemble – A Real Read. C.C. is retired from the slam competitive scene, but not before winning the 5th Annual Guild Complex Gwendolyn Brook's Open Mic Competition, and the Lambda Book Review's 1st Annual National Slam Competition at the Behind Our Mask Conference, as well as several local and national slams. She is an adjunct professor at Columbia College in Chicago where she teaches performance poetry workshops. She is currently the Program Director for an Adult Literacy and GED program in Chicago.